This book ~~belongs to:~~
is shared with

_____

_____

_____

the unicorn who found her magic

to all who quest

© June 2021 Conscious Stories LLC
Book 19

Illustrations Liesl Bell

Published by
Conscious Stories
350 E. Royal Lane
Suite #150
Irving, TX 75039

www.consciousstories.com

First Edition

ISBN 978-1-943750-54-2

Library of Congress
Control Number:
2021909170

The last 20 minutes of every day are precious.

Dear parents, teachers, and readers,

Although the realm of fairies and unicorns is often hidden from adults, it is frequently visible to children and adds great richness to their lives. When we validate their experience, we encourage their imagination, creativity, and playfulness. When we deny their experience, we create confusion and sadness. For the sensitive child, this is the difference between living open-hearted or closing down to protect themselves.

- Just because most grown-ups can't see it, doesn't change the fact that mystical worlds exist. The good news is that anyone can connect with unicorns, no matter their age.

- If you want to rediscover or explore the magical world of unicorns, practice **Alchemy's Magical Steps**, the exercise in the back of this book, to meet your personal unicorn. Bring your curiosity and openness and be willing to be surprised!

- Like all Conscious Stories, this book begins with the **Snuggle Breathing Meditation**™, a simple mindfulness practice to help you connect more deeply with your children in the last 20 minutes of each day.

(**Pro-tip:** Do the Unicorn meditation in nature, with your whole body connected to the earth.)

Enjoy snuggling into togetherness!

Andrew & Timea

An easy breathing meditation

Snuggle Breathing

Our story begins with us breathing together.
Say each line aloud and then
take a slow deep breath in and out.

I breathe for me

I breathe for you

I breathe for us

I breathe for all that surrounds us

AND

I breathe for all the unicorns!

Alchemy flew through whirlpools of stars,
over planets,
past a floating spaceman,
through pink fluffy clouds,
above majestic snow-capped mountains
(where dragons live),

8

and passed an airplane
... on her way to Earth.

After days of flying,
she landed in a beautiful forest.

Alchemy looked around curiously.
She pointed her horn
towards a tree, hoping it would
grow heart-shaped apples.

"Oopsie.

That's not my special magic."

Next, she waded into the ocean,
curious to see if she could
make starfish sparkle...

14

"I'm so sorry,"
she said, galloping away.

"Every mistake I make
has such bright, pretty colors.
I bet **my** special magic is
making sparkling rainbows"

She flew high into the sky
and pointed her horn at
a pink fluffy cloud.

"Oh no!
Rainbow-heart-shaped-
starfish-apples?"

21

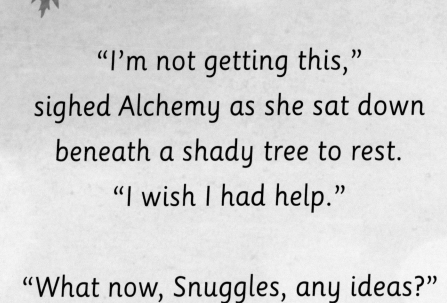

"I'm not getting this,"
sighed Alchemy as she sat down
beneath a shady tree to rest.
"I wish I had help."

"What now, Snuggles, any ideas?"

Before Snuggles had a chance
to answer, a voice whispered
from high up in the tree.

"Are you rrr-real?" asked a little
girl from her hiding place.

"You can see me?!"
replied Alchemy surprised.

"Oh my gosh. I'm talking to a unicorn!"
exclaimed the little girl excitedly.

"What are you doing here?"

26

"I'm looking for my special
kind of magic," sighed Alchemy.

"I've looked and looked,
but I can't find it anywhere.

I feel sad, tired and lonely,
and I don't feel very magical."

27

"You are the most magical thing
I've ever seen!" exclaimed the little girl.

"I was also feeling sad and lonely.
That's why I was hiding in the tree.
I feel happier just talking to you."

"I'm coming down to give you
a hug. You really helped me."

"But I didn't actually **do** anything!" exclaimed Alchemy.

"Yes you did. You sat with me
and talked to me, and now
I feel so much better."

Maybe **that's** your special magic:
helping kids feel happy,"
she said with a twinkle in her eye.

"That's it!" exclaimed Alchemy,
sparkling brighter than ever.
"You helped me find my magic."

"It's so easy!"

"All I have to do is
Be Myself."

Meet your unicorn

Alchemy's Magical Steps

Everybody has their very own unicorn. Would you like to meet yours?

Follow Alchemy's magical steps to make your special connection.

Invite your Unicorn

Whisper quietly... "I'd like to connect with my Unicorn."

2

1

Open your heart

Put your hand on your heart, close your eyes, and picture a bubble of shimmering white light around you. Breathe in love and breathe out peace.

Begin connecting

Picture your unicorn bowing its head, and light shining from the horn into your heart. Welcome the love flowing into you. How does it feel?

Listen curiously

Listen with your heart to what your unicorn has to tell you. Do you hear any words, see any pictures or feel something change in your body?

See with your inner eye

Imagine a sparkling rainbow light moving towards you as your magnificent unicorn appears.

Share what you discovered

Tell mom, dad, a friend, or write it down.

the growing collection

consciousstories

raising mindful **kids**

the forgetful
elephant

the prayer who
searched
for God

Andrew Newman

a little light

Andrew Newman

the sunburnt
polar bear

Andrew Newman

the unicorn
who found
her magic

the girl with
waterfall eyes

the boy who
searched
for silence

Andrew Newman

how diablo
became
Spirit

we are circle
people

the tree of
goodness

the elephant
who tried
to tiptoe

Rolling Thunder
finds his herd

Andrew Newman

the laughing
witch

the little
brain people

Andrew Newman

the hug who
got stuck

the bee who
could not choose
her flower

Andrew Newman
Illustrated by Marcella Mercit

the dad who
didn't know

the fish who
searched for
water

Andrew Newman
Illustrated by Marcella Mercit

ellie jumps
a mile

Andrew Newman

the home
for sensitive
butterflies

Andrew Newman

36

Consciousstories

A collection of stories with wise and lovable characters who teach spiritual values to your children

Helping you connect more deeply in the last 20 minutes of the day

Stories with purpose

Lovable characters who overcome life's challenges to find peace, love and connection.

Reflective activity pages

Cherish open sharing time with your children at the end of each day.

Simple mindfulness practices

Enjoy easy breathing practices that soften the atmosphere and create deep connection when reading together.

Supportive parenting community

Join a community of conscious parents who seek connection with their children.

Free downloadable coloring pages
Visit www.consciousstories.com

 #ConsciousBedtimeStories   @ConsciousBedtimeStories

Andrew Newman - author

Andrew Newman is the award-winning author and founder of www. ConsciousStories.com, a growing series of bedtime stories purpose-built to support parent-child connection in the last 20 minutes of the day. His professional background includes deep training in therapeutic healing work and mindfulness. He brings a calm yet playful energy to speaking events and workshops, inviting and encouraging the creativity of his audiences, children K-5, parents, and teachers alike.

Andrew has been an opening speaker for Deepak Chopra, a TEDx presenter in Findhorn, Scotland and author-in-residence at the Bixby School in Boulder, Colorado. He is a graduate of The Barbara Brennan School of Healing, a Non-Dual Kabbalistic healer and has b___ ___ively involved in men's work through the Mankind Project since 2___ ___ ___ parents, h___ ___ ___ return to their center, so they ca___ ___ent ___

Timea Kulcsar - au___

___ Kulcsar is a specialist ___ ___hor, and ___ ___cious ___ing. In 10 years of flow coaching, Timea has helped ___ of adults ___l from their childhood wounds. Along the way she learned the power ___ ___sence, the importance of connection, the essence of ease, and the joy ___honoring and accepting self. Now she brings these qualities to her first children's story, helping your little ones remember their own special magic.

Liesl Bell — illustrator

Born and raised in South Africa, Liesl moved to New York where she started her illustration career by creating corporate illustrations for IBM and Xerox's human resources intranet sites. Since then, she has had a line of hand-crafted greeting cards and illustrated numerous educational and private children's books, one of which awarded "This Book Rocks Award" for illustration. Her motto is: Create it with a smile and a wink. She now illustrates full-time in Jeffreys Bay, South Africa where she lives with her young son and two dogs.

www.zigglebell.com

Star Counter

Every time you breathe together and read aloud, you make a star shine in the night sky.

Color in a star to count how many times you have read this book.